W9-AWG-605

BERKLEY, the
Terrible Sleeper

By Mitchell Sharmat
Illustrated by Renée Kurilla

Ready-to-Read

Simon Spotlight

New York   London   Toronto   Sydney   New Delhi

SIMON SPOTLIGHT
An imprint of Simon & Schuster Children's Publishing Division
1230 Avenue of the Americas, New York, New York 10020
This Simon Spotlight edition September 2015
Text copyright © 2015 by Andrew Sharmat
Illustrations copyright © 2015 by Renée Kurilla
For information about special discounts for bulk purchases, please contact Simon &
Schuster Special Sales at 1-866-506-1949 or business@simonandschuster.com.
Manufactured in the United States of America 1015 LAK
10 9 8 7 6 5 4 3 2
Library of Congress Cataloging-in-Publication Data
Sharmat, Mitchell. Berkley, the terrible sleeper / by Mitchell Sharmat ; illustrated by
Renée Kurilla. — Simon Spotlight edition. pages cm. — (Ready-to-read)
Summary: "Most bears sleep all winter, but Berkley isn't most bears—he has trouble
falling asleep. Momma and Poppa Bear try to help, but nothing works. What will they
do if Berkley is still wide awake when winter comes?"— Provided by publisher.
[1. Bears—Fiction. 2. Bedtime—Fiction. 3. Sleep—Fiction.] I. Kurilla, Renée, illustrator.
II. Title. PZ7.S52992Be 2015 [E]—dc23 2014048494
ISBN 978-1-4814-3833-9 (hc)
ISBN 978-1-4814-3832-2 (pbk)
ISBN 978-1-4814-3834-6 (eBook)

Once upon a time
there were three bears.
No, not those three bears.
These were three other bears.
Poppa Bear, Momma Bear,
and little Berkley Bear.
"I'm a regular little bear
in a regular bear family,"
Berkley liked to say proudly.

But that wasn't quite true.
Unlike most bears,
Berkley was a terrible sleeper.
Every night, in their cave,
Poppa Bear would yawn and say,
"Time for bed."
And Berkley would always say,
"I'm not tired."

In early fall, his parents
became worried.
"If Berkley can't sleep through
one night," Momma Bear said,
"how can he sleep until spring?"

At breakfast one morning
Poppa asked Berkley,
"What are your plans for winter?"
Berkley looked up from his cereal.
"Momma and I are going to bed
for the winter," Poppa explained.
"For the whole winter?" asked Berkley.
"That's what bears do," said Poppa.

When Berkley went
out to play,
Momma and Poppa
called the doctor
for advice.

"We need your help, Dr. Bruin," Poppa said. "Berkley doesn't want to go to bed for the winter." "Get him a copy of my book, *Sleepy-Time Sloth Stories*," said Dr. Bruin. "It will put anyone to sleep!"

That night, Momma and Poppa
gave the book to Berkley
and went to bed.
They could hear him laughing
as he stayed up all night
reading about sloths.

The next morning
Berkley asked Momma,
"Why are sloths so sleepy?
I don't need much sleep at all."
"We know," said Poppa.
"So much for sleepy sloths,"
Momma groaned.

Winter kept getting closer,
so Poppa and Momma
kept trying to help.
"Let's take him to a concert,"
said Momma. "Violin music
is kind of like a lullaby."

The music was like a lullaby . . .
for Poppa and Momma Bear.
They fell asleep! Berkley did not.
He tapped his back paws
and clapped his front paws.
He shouted, "Bravo!"
and woke up Momma.
"So much for concerts," she said.

Soon, snow started to fall.
It was time for most bears
to go to sleep for the winter.
Momma and Poppa
tucked Berkley into bed.
"Berkley," they said, "here is
your winter hug and kiss.
See you in the spring."

Berkley tried to settle down.
"I can't sleep!" he soon cried out.
Poppa droned, "Tell yourself,
'My head is getting heavy.
My eyes are getting heavy.
My legs are getting heavy.
My stubby tail is getting heavy.'"
Berkley still tossed and turned.

Poppa said, "You want a glass
of water, right?"
"Wrong," Berkley answered.
Momma said, "You want us
to read you a story, right?"
"Wrong," Berkley answered.
"You want us to check under your bed
for the Big Bad Skunk?" Poppa asked.

"No water, no story, no skunk,"
Berkley said, shaking his head.
Momma Bear yawned.
She turned to Poppa.
"I suppose we could start
winter tomorrow night," she said.
"What's another night?" he agreed.
So they stayed up with Berkley.

The next day Poppa called Dr. Bruin.
"Huh, what?" groaned Dr. Bruin.
"Sorry to wake you," said Poppa,
"but Berkley still isn't sleepy."

"I'm afraid he might stay up
all winter," Dr. Bruin yawned.
"Leave him lots of things to do
and lots of food to eat. And please
don't call me until spring."
Poppa thanked the doctor.
Then he bought games, books, and
a cave-wall coloring set for Berkley.

Meanwhile, Momma made
four hundred honey sandwiches.

They carried everything
to Berkley's room and
kissed him on the forehead.
"Have a happy winter," yawned Poppa.
"Have a sleepy winter," yawned Momma.
And they went to bed.

Berkley wasn't sleepy.
So he played some games.
Then he painted on the walls
with his coloring set.
But he still wasn't sleepy.

Berkley sighed. "As long as I'm up,
maybe I can learn something."
He picked up a book about dancing
and began to read.

In December he learned to dance on all four paws.

In January he learned to dance on his two back paws.

In February he learned to dance
on his two front paws.
All the while,
Poppa and Momma slept on.

Finally, the snow melted,
and spring arrived.
Poppa and Momma Bear
sat up in bed and stretched.

When they got up,
they found Berkley asleep!
"What a good little bear!"
Momma whispered.
"He fell asleep in his own way."

Ten days later, Berkley woke up.
"What do you want to do today?"
asked Poppa.
"I want to show you what I learned
over the winter," said Berkley.

Berkley danced
on all four paws,

he danced on
two back paws,

and he danced on
two front paws.

"Guess what?"
Berkley said.
"After I learned to
dance, my stubby
tail got tired,

my legs got tired,

and then I
got tired and
fell asleep!"

Poppa looked at Momma.
Momma looked at Poppa.
"Did he just need to dance
all along?" Momma asked.
They both looked at Berkley.
The next day, they took Berkley
to his first dance class.

Soon, he was a star!
"That's our little bear!"
Momma said to Poppa.
"Turns out Berkley was born
to perform!" Poppa said proudly.
"And to sleep!" Momma added.
As long as he danced, Berkley
never had trouble sleeping again!